Archie's

Lewis and Daniil Owens

"I really enjoyed 'Archie's Way': it's a lovely story about why emotions, history and the Tube matter. Most of all, it's about how to be kind. I'd recommend it to any family, but especially to those whose lives are touched by autism."
Richard Ashcroft, Professor of Bioethics, Queen Mary University of London

"'Archie's Way' is a delightful and poignant read, reminding us that not all children think the same way. Funny, moving and historical, with some entertaining references to West Ham! Highly recommended!"
Baroness Karren Brady

"There are many wonderful children's stories out there today and 'Archie's Way' is certainly one of them. Not only does it entertain and educate the reader, it also reminds us that kindness is one of children's most innate and noble traits, regardless of how they look or think. With all proceeds going to a relevant charity, I cannot recommend this book highly enough."
Suzi Digby (Lady Eatwell) OBE

"I thoroughly enjoyed 'Archie's Way', a heart-warming story about a boy and his Dad on their somewhat unique adventures on the London Underground. It's a delightful read, crammed full of facts that will delight history and Tube buffs alike. It's a story about connection, humour, and kindness, but what I loved most is the way it embraces the idea that it's absolutely okay to be different. I can't wait for the next instalment!"
Lynne Laverty, Director of Autism Services at Centre for ADHD and Autism Support

Acknowledgements

This story is the result of blood, sweat, tears and several Tube journeys. We took our initial inspiration from the indefatigable Geoff Marshall and his enthusiasm for the London Tube Challenge. In a moment of madness, Dani and I decided it would be 'fun' to embark upon such a challenge. Little did we know how much planning would be involved (thanks, Mummy!) and equally how much stamina would be required. As I flagged half-way down the Piccadilly Line after five hours or so, Dani's energy increased - a testament both to him and his passion. He completed his first London Tube Challenge on September 1, 2014 in a remarkable time of 19 hours, 13 minutes and 5 seconds. Moreover, at the age of seven years, five months and 22 days we believe he still remains the youngest person on record to have completed the challenge. Just as importantly, he raised over £1000 for the charity Trekstock (www.trekstock.org.uk) who educate young people about avoidable cancer risks. From this 'moment of madness', the idea of 'Archie' was born.

While this is a fictional story, it is based on fact. There ARE remnants of a plague pit underneath where Aldgate Station now lies and people HAVE seen the Aldgate Ghost. Liverpool Street Station now rests on the site of the Old Bethlem Hospital and The Hoop and Grapes pub remains the oldest Public House in the City of London. I would like to thank the current landlord, Dan Walker, for taking me down to the cellars of the pub and relaying to me his own ghostly experiences...

Many people deserve thanks for helping this idea to become a reality. Alex Griffiths has been a wonderful source of encouragement, friendship, ideas and editing; Lee Oliver has also taken the time to make comments and suggestions, for which I am extremely grateful. Thanks are also due to Charlie and Toby Bruce, Richard and Nathan Lambert, Lars Martin Dahl, Angela and Daisy Teasdale, Robin and Madelaine Thompson, Terhi Manuel-Garner, Thomas Dixon, Richard Ashcroft and Mike Alsford. I would also like to acknowledge the kind messages of support we have received from Baroness Karren Brady, David Walliams, Tim Henman, Stephen Fry and Mark Haddon. Anna Robertson Davis has done a remarkable job with the illustrations and helped to bring the story to life.

Fortunately, there is continued and growing awareness of the autistic spectrum and how it affects children and adults in different ways. This is due in no small part to the incredible work of organisations like The Autism Research Trust, of which I am a proud Trustee, and we are delighted that all proceeds from this book will be donated to this important charity.

With thanks for reading and very best wishes,

Lewis and Daniil Owens
November 2018

For Mummy and Sofia

CHAPTER 1

By the time Archie's Dad had finally found his keys, the taxi had already been purring like a kitten outside 10 Star Crescent for over three minutes.

"Dad! Are you coming?" roared 11-year-old Archie, waiting by the front door, his rucksack slung expectantly over his shoulder and a worried look on his face. "We're going to be late!"

"Yes, got them. Coming. Don't shout. You'll wake your Mum and sister," replied Archie's Dad, wrapping his West Ham United scarf tightly round his neck and quietly closing the door behind him.

It was extremely dark outside and very cold. As Archie and his Dad climbed into the taxi, the driver gave them a rather puzzled look.

"Bit early, innit? I mean, 4.30am? Where you off to? Heathrow or Gatwick?" the driver asked, stretching his rather thick neck to face his passengers.

"Chesham station," replied Archie immediately. "We are doing the London Tube Challenge."

"What's that then?" asked the driver, confused. "I normally just do the airport runs."

"The London Tube Challenge means that we have to pass through all 270 Underground stations as fast as we can. We are starting from Chesham. The world record is 15 hours, 45 minutes and 38 seconds," explained Archie.

"Oh," said the taxi driver, still puzzled. "Why are you doing that?"

"Why not?!" came Archie's immediate reply. "I know all of the different Tube routes, lines and stations in my head. It will be great fun."

"Fair enough," said the driver, adjusting his sat nav and frowning to himself. "Chesham station it is."

Archie had been interested in trains for as long as he could remember. There was something about their predictable routes and timings that made him feel comfortable and safe from the unpredictable world outside. Trains came at certain, agreed times: 05:15, 05:45, 06:15.... Perfect! He liked that. In fact, Archie loved *all* kinds of numbers and dates: train and bus timetables, tennis scores, Roman gods and goddesses and sightings of the planet Venus. What Archie *didn't* like was being late. Or sudden noises. Or bright lights. Or dogs: big ones, small ones, smart ones, scruffy ones, smelly ones or perfumed ones.

But most of all Archie liked Felicity Fishmonger. Felicity was in Archie's class at school. To Archie she seemed really cool. Unfortunately it seemed that Felicity didn't feel the same way about Archie. In fact, she felt he was a nerd (only Archie would know the name of a thirty-two sided polygon, she thought, and in fact she wasn't even sure what a polygon was). He knew that it was unlikely that she would come to his birthday party. He hadn't received a reply yet but he wasn't holding his breath (and he knew that the world record for holding one's breath was 24 minutes and 3 seconds and he didn't want to try and beat that).

As he looked out of the taxi window and noticed the planet Venus shining bright, Archie couldn't help thinking that Felicity was, deep down, a good person. He thought good things about everyone, even his Dad, who could be *so* annoying by singing awful songs and telling even worse jokes. He turned to look at his Dad, who was busy with a large folder that listed the exact route they needed to take, which would have them ending up at Heathrow Terminal 5 shortly before midnight at the end of their Challenge. "Dad finds it difficult to just manage that folder," thought Archie to himself, "but my mind seems busier than the London Underground - my thoughts are always starting, stopping and connecting!"

"I had Tim Henman in the back of my cab last week," said the taxi driver, proudly breaking the silence.

"Oh..." said Archie's Dad, looking up from his folder, unsure how to respond.

Archie was impressed: "He got to the semi-final of

Wimbledon four times: 1998, 1999, 2001 and 2002. At one point he was ranked No. 4 in the world."

"Did he....was he..." replied Archie's Dad, pretending to be as impressed as Archie.

Twenty minutes, seventeen questions and two Abba songs on the radio later, they arrived.

"Here we are: Chesham Station. That's £19.80 please, guv," said the driver checking the fare.

"Thank you very much. Keep the change," said Archie's Dad kindly, handing over a £20 note.

"Oh, ta..." said the driver, not very impressed with the size of the tip. "I forgot to tell you about Kylie Minogue. I've had 'er in the back seat too."

"Next time," said Archie's Dad. "We must make this train!"

CHAPTER 2

After searching for his Oyster card in a panic, finding it, and then dropping it twice, Archie's Dad followed his son onto the platform where they climbed onto the 05:15 train heading to Watford.

They both sat down with a huge sigh of relief. The carriage was empty. Not surprising, thought Archie's Dad, as most sensible people would still be tucked up in bed at this time of the morning. He checked the schedule in his folder, worried about missing anything; Archie checked his watch instead. "Any second," he said excitedly.

A voice came over the speakers: "Mind the gap between the train and the platform. This is Chesham. The next station is Chalfont & Latimer. This is a Metropolitan line train to Watford."

Soon enough, they were on the move. Archie felt a mix of fun and fear. He had been looking forward to this day for weeks, ever since his Dad suggested as a joke that they could beat the world record. But Archie was very serious: they *could* break the record with enough planning, desire and, of course, a little good luck (and no delays!).

"I wonder if we will see Einstein," said Archie, looking back out of the window into the dark winter morning.

"Einstein?" said his Dad, perplexed. "Is he the Metropolitan Line cat?"

"Dad, don't be silly. Einstein is a machine engine that helps during engineering work. You can see it on Platform 3," said Archie.

"Bit of a funny name. I mean, why Einstein? I would call it Bonds or Devonshire or Brooking or-" said Archie's Dad, remembering all of his favourite West Ham players.

"Dad!" interrupted Archie. "It's called Einstein."

"OK, OK," nodded Archie's Dad.

The train continued out towards Rickmansworth.

"Hang on!" cried Archie's Dad suddenly, flipping frantically through his folder. "We look like we're heading *away* from London. That can't be right! Oh help..."

"It's only Rickmansworth, Dad," replied Archie, noticing the concern on his Dad's face. "In the old days," he explained, "people would change here before carrying on their journey into Buckinghamshire by steam."

"Buckinghamshire?!" replied Archie's Dad with more concern. "I hope we don't end up too far in the countryside! I thought this is supposed to be the *London* Tube Challenge. We will never finish it by midnight if we end up too far in the sticks," he continued, looking at his folder again before checking something on his phone.

But Archie wasn't worried. He decided not to bother telling his Dad that the London Underground actually also went out to Essex and Hertfordshire, as well as Buckinghamshire and Middlesex, or that if you put all the tracks together, they covered a total of 250 miles. 250 miles! That was longer than the distance from London to Liverpool! In fact, Archie had read somewhere that in the 1890s the Metropolitan Railway went as far as 50 miles north of Baker Street, past Aylesbury to Verney Junction!

London was *much* bigger than he had first thought and certainly much bigger now than the London Wall constructed by the Romans centuries ago. Archie had learnt about the Romans at school but had read more about them by himself at home. He knew that the Wall had had several gates to let people in and out of the City: Ludgate, Newgate, Bishopsgate and his favourite one, Aldgate. It was his favourite because it was still an active Underground station (even though the original Old Gate – after which Aldgate was named – was demolished in 1760 and now Boots the Chemist was there instead!).

Archie understood that his knowledge and his rather unusual thoughts were his own, and that his Dad would be surprised by what he knew, and impressed, yes – but ultimately, his Dad just couldn't store information the way Archie could. As he had told the taxi driver, he knew all of the Tube line stations and connections off by heart and could picture them in his mind as clearly as any book or map. It was Archie's gift – one of them, anyway.

CHAPTER 3

"Four times!" said Archie's Dad suddenly, with an air of surprise.

"What?" said Archie, confused.

"Tim Henman. He got to the semi-final of Wimbledon four times."

"I told you that already, Dad. He also got to the semi-final of the French Open and the US Open in 2004," said Archie immediately, as he carried on looking out of the window thinking how the shadowy trees looked like ginormous people.

Archie's Dad continued to look at his phone, nodding to himself when he realised that Archie had the facts exactly right, as always.

By the time the train arrived at Watford, the carriage was much fuller, with people starting their commute to work, spilling their coffee and putting on their make-up. Archie's Dad leaned over to Archie as they headed for the exit: "Hey, listen to this," he said clearing his throat. Speaking very loudly so that everyone could hear, he announced: "Please mind the *Watford* Gap between the train and the platform!" and chuckled with laughter. The fellow passengers looked at him with a mixture of sympathy and confusion: one young woman thought about offering him some spare change; a rather glamorous lady smudged her lipstick up towards her nose while a young man in a smart suit cursed to himself as his café latte dribbled onto his white collar.

When they got off the train, their first train journey of many now complete, Archie said very firmly, "Dad, please don't EVER do that again."

"Oh, sorry. I thought it was quite good. You know, Watford Gap..."

"...No, Dad, it wasn't," interrupted Archie. "I heard that man over there say to his wife that I was obviously taking you to Watford General Hospital for a check-up."

"Check-up?"

"Luckily, Watford Station is going to close this year so you won't need to try that joke again...."

"Why is it closing? I bet Elton John won't be happy."

"Who?"

"Elton John. You know: the singer. Wears funny hats and wigs. He likes Watford. Well, the football club, mainly." Archie's Dad began badly singing to the tune of 'Candle in the Wind': "Goodbyyyeee, Watford Station, though I never kneeeeeew you at aaaaallllll..."

"Dad!" roared Archie.

"Sorry, son... So what will happen to the train we have just taken – the one from Chesham – if there won't be a Watford Station anymore?"

"Trains will be re-routed and the Metropolitan line

extended," replied Archie. "The MLE is due to open in 2020."

"Who's Emily?" asked Archie's Dad, confused.

"No, Dad, MLE – Metropolitan Line Extension. It will divert trains to new stations close to the football stadium."

"Oh, I see," said Archie's Dad, although it was clear he didn't really understand.

Archie sat patiently on the platform bench while they waited for the next train. As much as he loved his Dad and knew that he was very clever, he was aware that for a grown-up he really didn't know very much about trains. What was worse, his Dad's stomach was rumbling very loudly indeed. The final straw came when his Dad noticed 'Basil's Baguettes' on the opposite platform and licked his lips so loudly that other people turned to stare. It was even worse than the singing. "Dad!" said Archie, embarrassed and frustrated. "This is supposed to be a Challenge. We need to do it as quickly as possible. You don't have time for a bacon sandwich. We have to get to Harrow-on-the-Hill next. Quick! We have to catch the train."

CHAPTER 4

They made the train with about 30 seconds to spare after a last-minute platform change. Archie's Dad sat back heavily in his seat, his face as red as the Central Line, and breathed a huge sigh of relief.

"Hmmmnn," said Archie's Dad, thoughtfully after a minute or so. "I wonder if Winston Churchill ever got this train?"

"Winston Churchill?" asked Archie, a little confused as to why his Dad was now talking about the man who used to be Prime Minister years and years ago.

"Yes, I think he went to Harrow School. It's just by Harrow-on-the-Hill Tube station, where we're heading now. Perhaps he got the Tube to school. In fact, I remember reading somewhere that lots of famous people went there. It's probably on Wikipedia – hang on, I'll have a look," he said.

Archie's Dad started to scroll down on his phone and became quite excited. "Aha," he said, triumphantly, punching his arm in the air, startling Archie. "Daddy rocks! Churchill went to Harrow School and it says that he is one of six British Prime Ministers to have gone there," he said, scrolling down.

"I'm sure that that actor bloke went there, too," Archie's Dad continued. "You know, the good one. Played Sherlock Holmes. Lives at Baker Street. Your mum likes him. What's his name? Benjamin Cummerbund."

"You mean Benedict Cumberbatch, Dad," Archie said quietly.

"That's the one. Yes, look, it says it here," said Archie's Dad, reading his phone and punching his arm in the air once again. "Daddy rocks again!"

Archie looked embarrassed but quickly asked, "Did Tim Henman go there too?"

"No, not as far as I know. But funnily enough," said Archie's Dad, still looking at his phone, "according to Wikipedia, the very first two Wimbledon tennis champions did. Harrow's a very famous school – founded in 1672, I think. Very expensive, though. Ridiculously expensive, to be honest."

"It sounds like an amazing school," said Archie. "Can I go there?" he asked, curiously.

Archie's Dad's humour suddenly stopped and his face quickly went as grey as the Jubilee Line. "Well, it's not that good, actually, Archie. I don't think you'd like it. Very strict." He felt it best to change the subject, and quickly. "Uxbridge next," he said, checking his folder as his mobile phone rang suddenly.

Archie looked away, embarrassed again, as the theme to *Star Wars* on his Dad's phone filled the carriage on maximum volume. Archie's Dad answered the call, which was something about his work. Archie knew that his Dad, who was a Professor of Medieval History at the local university, was due to be going on a research trip to Iceland, an island full of history and volcanoes. Archie secretly hoped that his Dad would also take him if he wasn't at school.

Archie looked around him and suddenly his heart skipped a beat. Walking up the carriage, carrying a McDonalds take-away in her hand and a sour expression on her face, was none other than Felicity Fishmonger and her Mum. This early in the morning?! It was only 6.37am! They sat almost opposite Archie and his Dad without noticing them at first. Archie looked away and hoped he wouldn't be seen. But Felicity's eyes were sharp.

CHAPTER 5

"Oh, what a surprise," Felicity said to Archie in a mocking tone of voice, noticing that his Dad was busy talking on the phone. "Archie Balde is on the Underground. Have you been here all morning? It wouldn't surprise me if you sleep here," she laughed, glancing at her mother who was already engrossed in her Jackie Collins novel and unaware of anything else around her. Felicity leaned forward and whispered quietly, so that only Archie could hear:

Archie, Archie, as boring as a nerd
Archie, Archie, not worth being heard

Archie could feel the tears welling up and his face beginning to turn red. But he looked at her and asked with a voice that cracked only slightly with sadness, confusion and embarrassment:

"Why do you have to be so mean, Felicity?" he asked her softly. "I haven't done anything to you. I never call you names or tease you but you always seem to make fun of me. Why?"

"Because you are WEIRD," replied Felicity. "You memorise train connections and tennis results. You know what something with 32 sides is called and you can tell everyone *every single score from every single week of* Strictly Come Dancing. How weird is that?"

"But I like doing things like that," Archie replied, still in a soft voice. "It doesn't hurt you. Does it?"

Felicity hunted for an answer. "Well no, but it annoys me. And you always get the best scores in Maths. Teacher's pet." She pulled a face to show how annoying she found him.

"But I like Maths..." said Archie honestly.

"I even remember," Felicity continued at full steam, "when you stood up and told everyone in the class about the planet Venus. That every hundred years or so we can see it crossing the Sun, or something stupid like that. How can information like that *ever* be useful or interesting? Weird."

Archie looked down. He couldn't understand why anybody would *not* be interested in Venus. It was similar in many ways to our own planet Earth, particularly Iceland, and the Greeks and Romans named it after their goddesses of love and beauty. He wasn't sure quite what love and beauty were, really, but he was certain it didn't mean simply how someone looked on the outside. There must be more to love and beauty than that, he thought. He had seen some photos of Roman statues of the goddess Venus that had been discovered underground in London, but she looked so unnaturally perfect in them. Archie preferred the more recent sculpture of Venus that overlooked Liverpool Street Station at Broadgate: the face and hair actually reminded him a bit of Felicity. He didn't think Felicity would ever make the front cover of a beauty or fashion magazine, but he liked that. Even though she was so mean to him, Felicity was somehow cool in other ways. He couldn't quite explain it, but there was something about her that he felt was nice underneath it all. He hoped that she felt the same way about him – that underneath her meanness she actually liked him.

"Where are you going?" Archie asked, changing the subject, as Felicity was tucking into her Egg McMuffin.

"We're going to visit my great uncle," she replied, wiping a dribble of egg from her chin.

"Where does he live?" asked Archie.

"Duh, stupid. He's buried in Highgate cemetery," came her reply.

"Oh, sorry. I didn't know," said Archie, looking down again.

Archie was tempted to tell Felicity how the names of Highgate and Archway had changed over time: Archway was originally called Highgate, then renamed Archway (Highgate) then Highgate (Archway) before staying as Archway as it is today, but he decided against it.

"He would have been 100 years old today," continued Felicity, with a surprising tone of sensitivity in her voice.

"Wow," replied Archie, as he quickly calculated that Felicity's great uncle must have been born in 1917, when the First World War meant there was no Wimbledon Tennis Championship and over 300,000 people used London Underground stations as shelters from German bombs.

"He was only 11 when he died," added Felicity, "the same age as we are now."

"That's really young. How did he die?" asked Archie.

"My mum said he drowned in a really bad flood in London," replied Felicity.

Archie knew that the River Thames often flooded in the olden days but didn't know many details. He made a mental note to read up about it when he got home. He knew already that the River Thames ran for about 215 miles but that there were also lots of streams still running underneath the surface of the City. London was really like a giant person who was never still but always moving. He looked down at a scar on his hand, which he had got when he was just three and had slipped and cut himself on a shard of glass. Just like the River Thames, he thought, the blood underneath the skin sometimes breaks the surface.

This was the first time that Archie and Felicity had had a *proper* conversation. Archie could feel his heart pumping fast to the click-click rhythm of the train and he thought carefully about what to say next.

"You still have some egg on your chin," he pointed out, honestly and bluntly.

Felicity blushed and quickly grabbed a tissue. She didn't seem particularly happy with Archie's last comment so he tried again.

"Trains from here to Archway always arrive on platform 4," he said.

"Do you know *everything* about trains?" asked Felicity, now egg-free.

"Not *everything*," replied Archie, smiling, "but most things."

"But doesn't it bore you? I mean, just learning numbers and dates and connections," she asked.

"No, I like it," he replied.

"Weird," said Felicity to herself as she finished her breakfast.

"And I like you as well, even though you don't like me," he thought to himself, "even with egg on your chin."

CHAPTER 6

As they continued on their journey Felicity suddenly became very nervous, looking out of the window with a worried expression on her face.

"What's wrong?" asked Archie, concerned and noticing her unease.

"Baker Street station. It's coming up soon and I remember it has tunnels. I hate tunnels and we have to stay underground until we get off at King's Cross," she said, with her voice trembling slightly.

Archie was pleasantly surprised by Felicity's knowledge of the tunnels, but equally surprised that she would be so scared of them. She didn't seem to be afraid of anything at school, not even when Harry Hornrimm brought in his pet tarantula to show the class.

"Would you like to look at my book until you get to King's Cross and out of the tunnel?" asked Archie, thoughtfully. "I don't mind, and it might take your mind off being scared," he said, taking out his rather battered copy of *Demon Dentist* and offering it to her. "I have read it three times already. It's very funny. Would you like some apple juice, too?"

Felicity took the book and the bottle of apple juice that Archie was offering her from out of his rucksack. She looked at the pictures, mainly just to forget about being inside a tunnel, and she was grateful for the distraction.

"Felicity, come on. King's Cross next," came the voice of Felicity's Mum, rising and beckoning her daughter to follow.

Felicity closed the book and looked relieved. "Thank you," she said to Archie, with a slightly more friendly voice. "I've never told anyone before that I don't like tunnels."

"That's OK," said Archie, his mind whirling into action, "57% of the London Underground is actually overground, so it's not all tunnels. And Baker Street has 10 platforms, which is the most of any station. In 1863, when the Metropolitan Railway opened..."

But Felicity was already out of the door with her Mum, shaking her head and quietly singing:

Archie, Archie....

Archie felt himself blush and was grateful that the doors were already closing, meaning that he didn't have to sit and feel any more embarrassed than he already was. She had left with his book and his bottle of apple juice but he didn't mind. He would see her at school tomorrow. More importantly, they had talked. Properly! Yes, she was singing the rhyme again about him being a nerd because of all the facts about the Underground, but they had had a real conversation too. Deep down, despite Felicity's cruelty, he was pleased, and his heart was pumping as strong as the River Thames.

"So, the next destination is Euston," said Archie's Dad suddenly, no longer on the phone and now looking back through his folder. "According to my schedule we should be there in two minutes. We are still on track to visit all the stations in one day. Literally – *on track*," he laughed aloud. "Get it?! We're 'on track' meaning that we're on time, and we're on a *train track*!"

"I know, Dad," said Archie, quietly. His Dad was embarrassing with his cheesy jokes, but that didn't matter to Archie right then. He was still thinking about his conversation with Felicity.

CHAPTER 7

"1572," came the voice, suddenly, of a man sitting opposite.

"I'm sorry?" replied Archie's Dad, looking up to see who had spoken.

"1572," repeated the man. "Forgive me, but I couldn't help overhearing your conversation about Harrow School earlier. It was actually founded in 1572, not 1672."

"I see," said Archie's Dad, a little put out. "Er, well, thank you for the correction." To be honest, each of them had sort of forgotten that they'd ever had that conversation: Archie's Dad had been distracted by his work phone-call, and Archie himself had been dealing with Felicity, of course.

"Not at all," said the man, evidently delighted that Archie's Dad had replied to him. "Reeves," he continued, holding out a rather dirty-looking hand in the direction of Archie's Dad, "my name is Eugene Reeves."

As Archie's Dad looked at this Reeves fellow, he wondered how he and Archie had managed not to notice him the moment they stepped onto the Tube train – or, for that matter, how no-one else sat around them seemed to have noticed either. Was he seeing things? It was an extraordinary sight: Reeves was wearing clothes that did not seem to belong either to the current times or to his build. He wore a white cotton shirt with frayed edges and the most *enormous* lace collar, and around that he was also wearing a worn-out scarf. He had long hair, a small beard and non-matching and very dirty socks – one blue, one white – which he wore outside green velvet trousers and which came up to his knees. He also smelt funny.

"James Balde," replied Archie's Dad, politely yet tentatively extending his own hand to meet that of his new companion, "and my son Archie."

Archie's Dad looked at his son, trying to reassure him in case he was afraid of this strange man opposite them who looked like he belonged in a museum. Archie, though, whilst a little wide-eyed at the marvel before him, didn't seem overly concerned. Archie was the kind of boy who took an interest in others and accepted them as they were, without being too worried about different or unusual features. Archie's Dad admired that in his son.

"Delighted to meet you both," continued Reeves, stroking his beard. "Do I take it from what you were saying that you are planning to visit all of the London Underground stations in one day?"

"Yes!" exclaimed Archie, with great excitement. "It's called the London Tube Challenge and we have to pass through -"

"I know, young man. I know," interrupted Reeves with a smile. "I know only too well."

"You've done it yourself?" asked Archie's Dad, with a certain scepticism.

"Mainly just the Metropolitan Line." replied Reeves. "I have some personal business to attend to and so I regularly travel back and forth between the 14 stations that link Harrow-on-the-Hill and Aldgate."

"Wow!" exclaimed Archie. "This is our first time we have tried the Challenge."

"I see. No school today, then?" asked Reeves.

"Inset day," exclaimed Archie's Dad quickly, knowing how strange school inspectors can look. He wasn't taking any chances. "Day off. No school."

CHAPTER 8

Soon, Reeves and Archie were engrossed in a conversation about all sorts of topics. Reeves was increasingly impressed with Archie's knowledge: he knew more about the Underground than any boy that he had ever met. Archie's Dad, on the other hand, couldn't help but feel somewhat left out and, quite frankly, a little cross with this new, knowledgeable and rather mysterious travel companion. "I bet he doesn't know anything about Tim Henman or Benjamin Cummerbund, though," he said under his breath as he hunted in vain through his pockets for his Oyster card.

As the train continued towards the next part of their Tube Challenge, Archie's Dad's energy had already begun to plummet. "I knew I should have had that bacon sandwich," he muttered to himself as he peered rather unimpressed at his packed lunch, trying to work out whether the strong smell came from his salami sandwiches or from Mr Reeves. He concluded it was from both. He put the sandwiches back in his bag and settled for a banana.

Meanwhile, Reeves and Archie were still engaged in a lively discussion, seemingly unaware of the increasing number of people entering the train. Archie's Dad listened to the conversation, which was becoming more and more strange.

"As I say, I have been around a long time and seen many things," Reeves was saying. "In fact, believe it or not, I was born in the year 1600."

Archie's Dad couldn't help laughing out loud. "1600?" he said. "Goodness. I know the delays have been rather bad recently, but 400 years is a huuuuuuge delay. You really should speak to Transport for London and ask for your money back," he chuckled, looking at Archie.

But Archie wasn't smiling. Rather, he was looking at Mr Reeves with utter fascination.

"How can you have been born in 1600?" said Archie, confused. "Are you a time-traveller? Or a ghost? Or just very, very old? I don't understand."

"Yes, it does sound extraordinary," Reeves admitted, "but I am indeed a ghost. The ghost of Eugene Reeves. And I need some help. I have to tell you a story first in order for you to understand. Then you can help me solve a riddle. Let me try to explain."

CHAPTER 9

As the Underground train continued on the Metropolitan Line, this deeply mysterious man Reeves started to tell Archie how he was once the Landlord of *The Castle* pub in Aldgate. He used to live there with his wife in a small attic room and it suited them perfectly. It was small but cosy, and most importantly it was their *home*.

"I bet you were never late for work either!" joked Archie's Dad.

Reeves smiled politely and continued with his story.

"Have you heard of the Great Plague, Archie?" he asked.

"Yes, definitely," replied Archie, remembering his school lessons on that horrible subject. He told Reeves that he knew how it started in 1664 because of dirty rats spreading disease and by the time it was over in 1665 it had killed over 100,000 people.

"100,000 people!" exclaimed Archie's Dad. "My goodness! That's the same number as two completely full West Ham Stadiums."

"Dad, do you have to relate *everything* to West Ham?" moaned Archie. "It's really boring sometimes."

Archie's Dad looked a little upset but decided not to reply. Anyway, even if he had wanted to he wouldn't have had the chance as Reeves was speaking again.

"It was such a horribly sad time," Reeves said. "Many people were buried in horrible, disgusting ditches – or 'plague pits' as they were called. Did you know that Aldgate Station was built on top of one of the biggest ones?"

"You mean that there are actually people buried underneath Aldgate station?" asked Archie, astonished. He had a vague memory of a story on the news that said some archaeological remains had recently been discovered, but he couldn't remember where.

"That is exactly what I mean," answered Reeves. "That's where my wife Bertha and I ended up," said Reeves, sadly.

"*You had the Plague?*" asked Archie, his eyes wide open. "*You died? Of the Plague?*"

"Yes, my wife and I both died," continued the sad ghost, addressing Archie.

"No wonder you stink," thought Archie's Dad to himself, before saying out loud, "Archie, I really think we should move to a different carriage."

"But Dad, Mr Reeves says he needs help. We can't leave him," said Archie with a hopeful, pleading look in his eyes.

"The Tube Challenge, Archie!" replied his Dad. "That's the whole reason we're here. We will have to get off the train soon if we are to stay on schedule."

Reeves knew that he would have to persuade Archie and his Dad to stay and help him. He had the feeling that Archie's Dad didn't believe much of what he was saying. He had to convince them, especially Archie's Dad, and quickly!

"Mr Balde," he started, "I will prove to you that what I am saying is the complete and honest truth."

"Oh, yes?" said Archie's Dad, not taking Reeves very seriously. "And how will you do that?"

"I want to take you to my old home, where I used to be Landlord," he answered.

"You mean *The Castle*, where you lived in the attic with your wife?" asked Archie.

"Exactly, Archie," replied Reeves.

"Ha ha ha! You cannot be serious!" laughed Archie's Dad. "Why on earth would we leave the train with someone who claims to be a ghost from the 17th Century and dresses worse than Captain Underpants! This is more hilarious than *Eastenders*!"

"Mr Balde, please just listen to me. Please," begged Reeves.

"Dad!" pleaded Archie. "Please!"

"OK, OK, I am listening, Mr Reeves," Archie's Dad replied, leaning back in his chair. If anything, he said it just to calm them down, as he was afraid that people on the train would start looking at them strangely if Reeves and Archie got much louder. "Do continue with your, um, er, interesting story."

"Thank you," said Reeves, composing himself, for he looked a little upset. "I need you to find someone very important to me."

"Your hairdresser?" said Archie's Dad with a chuckle, looking at his companion's rather long and dirty hair.

"No, Mr Balde, not my hairdresser," said Reeves firmly. "I need you to help me find my wife."

CHAPTER 10

Those words seemed to shock Archie's Dad, who sat up slightly and looked a little embarrassed.

"Oh, I see. Well, um, OK, right. Sorry," he stuttered. He still had no idea how any of this made any sense.

Reeves realised that he now had Archie's Dad's attention and wasted no time in explaining further. "As I mentioned earlier," he started, "my wife and I both died in that awful Plague. When we first passed into the ghostly world we were together all the time but at some point we became separated. I simply cannot find her anymore and London is full of ghosts bumping and barging into each other. It's sometimes more crowded than rush hour on the Underground."

"I doubt that," thought Archie's Dad to himself, remembering the many times when his nose had been pressed into strangers' armpits on the Central Line.

"I haven't seen my wife for over 100 years," continued Reeves, "but I know that she must be close by."

"How do you know?" asked Archie. "Have other ghosts seen her?"

"It's not the other ghosts that have seen her," said Reeves rather mysteriously, "but living people."

"What on earth do you mean?" asked Archie's Dad.

"There have been many reports of a ghost being spotted at Aldgate Station. She is called the 'Elderly Angel' with silvery hair. Apparently she helps various people who have got into difficulties. I know it must be her. She was always such a kind, helpful lady."

"You mean to say that you think she has gone back to the horrible plague pit you were thrown into when you died? The one underneath Aldgate Station?" Archie asked, his mind in a whirl.

"Yes, Archie, that is exactly what I mean."

Archie was trying to process everything Reeves had told him. What could it all mean? It sounded so incredible that it hardly seemed possible, and yet there was something about this strange man that made him seem like someone you could trust. Archie felt that the story simply must be true, no matter how extraordinary it sounded. Archie's Dad was also slowly beginning to wonder if there was something in this bizarre story. He began to listen more seriously, frowning and biting his lip.

"But how can *we* help?" asked Archie.

"As I said before, I need you to help me solve a riddle. I have tried myself but I simply cannot find the answer. I need someone with your unique mind, Archie. A mind that finds connections with dates and numbers that most people miss," Reeves said.

Archie frowned. He knew that he thought differently to most 11-year-olds but he never thought he was special enough to solve a riddle to help a ghost! But, why not?! If he could help Reeves, he would gladly do so. No-one at school would believe him, of course (except maybe Harry Hornrimm, who once claimed in assembly that he was the brother of Buzz Lightyear).

"OK, I will try my best to help," said Archie very seriously. "What do I have to do?"

Reeves smiled with relief. "Come with me to the cellars of *The Castle*," he continued. "That's where the riddle is. From there I am sure you will be able to help me solve the meaning of it and help me to find my wife. I will explain exactly what I mean if you will only agree to come with me and help me."

Archie and his Dad looked at each other, not knowing what to say.

Reeves could see that they were concerned. "I know that you are worried about your Tube Challenge," he said, "but I promise you I can ensure that you won't lose any time. One of the benefits of being a ghost, apart from the fact that only very few people can see you, is that we are not controlled by the normal rules of time and space, even those declared by Einstein."

Archie's Dad suddenly piped up: "Einstein. Platform 3. Metropolitan Line. Helps with engineering works." He smiled with satisfaction, believing he had out-smarted his companion.

"Not *that* Einstein, Mr Balde," replied Reeves, looking back at Archie, who was shaking his head with embarrassment. "Albert Einstein, the famous scientist who made great discoveries about time and space."

Archie's Dad rolled his eyes and wondered if he would ever understand this ghost Reeves. "So what are you trying to say now?"

Reeves continued. "I have been waiting for someone to help me all these years, and I think you are the one, Archie. You and your father are the only people not in the ghostly world who have been able to see me with your eyes for over 350 years. To everyone else I am invisible. To me, this means you see reality differently and more deeply than other people. What's more, Archie," he continued, looking across with a sort of amusement and pity, "despite his terrible sense of humour and singing, your Dad can also see me which means he must also have *some* qualities... You will both be able to help me. Please. At the moment I have nowhere to call my home."

"Dad, yes!" pleaded Archie.

"Well, I don't really... Archie," stuttered his Dad before stopping, admitting to himself that he had slowly become extremely intrigued by the story that Reeves had told them. "If it's OK with Archie then I guess it's OK with me," he thought.

Reeves saw the hesitation on Archie's Dad's face and seized his chance.

"Mr Balde," he said, "I will show you shortly that in the ghostly world space and time are very different to how you experience them. I can promise you now that you will not lose a single second on your Tube Challenge."

Archie's Dad threw up his hands in resignation, forgetting he was holding his folder, which came down with a crash, startling Archie once more. "I knew I should have stayed in bed this morning," he said to himself, collecting the scattered papers from the floor. "OK, OK, fine! We will come with you," he said, finally. "I just hope I don't regret this."

"Wonderful!" exclaimed Reeves, clearly relieved and excited that Archie and his Dad had agreed to help him. He spoke quickly, before they could change their minds." We will need to get off at Aldgate Station, the next stop. *The Castle* is very close to the exit but is now called by a different name: *The Hoop and Grapes*. I will of course be invisible but you will need to slip down secretly into the cellars without anyone seeing you. Once we are there no one will bother us and I will tell you the riddle."

Archie's Dad couldn't believe that he had agreed to get *off* the Tube because of this man wearing green velvet trousers, dirty, smelly socks and a huge lace collar. They were never going to complete the Challenge at this rate! It was true that no-one else outside seemed to notice Reeves, though. "Maybe he really is a ghost," thought Archie's Dad. "But he can't be... Can he?"

CHAPTER 11

Archie, his Dad and Reeves came out of Aldgate station and made their way towards the public house where Reeves claimed that he and his wife used to live. Archie felt nervous: Reeves had said that he needed Archie's mind to help him to find his wife, and he didn't want to let his new ghost friend down. It seemed like a big responsibility. Still, at least his Dad was with him. Archie looked up: his Dad was looking puzzled, as if he could hardly believe what was happening, but when he saw Archie gazing up at him with a worried expression on his face, he smiled reassuringly at his son. Archie took hold of his Dad's hand for extra comfort. He was excited, yes, but nervous too. Would they be able to help Reeves? And would they really still be able to complete the Tube Challenge without losing any time?

Archie could see the place where Reeves used to live a little further down and across the road. To Archie's unique way of thinking, the building looked rather like his English teacher, Mr Penfold: tall, thin, leaning slightly to the side with a small, pointed head where the attic obviously was. In front was a large sign: THE HOOP AND GRAPES.

The three unusual companions – an 11-year-old boy, his Dad, and a 17th-Century ghost - paused outside the entrance. Reeves suggested that he should enter first as he would be invisible. After two or three minutes Archie and his Dad should then enter and politely ask if Archie could use the toilet. The toilet! Archie giggled at that one. Reeves noticed and explained kindly that yes, it sounded funny, but it was the easiest way of getting down to the cellar without seeming suspicious: the toilet was right next to the cellar entrance, after all. By the time Archie and his Dad had made their way down, Reeves would have unlocked the door to the cellar and Archie and his Dad would quickly head over to him, with Reeves locking the door behind them.

It all worked perfectly. Within five minutes of getting off the Tube, they were all in the cellar. It was predictably dark, despite being lit with long fluorescent lights. Numerous pipes and funnels ran from the ceiling into different barrels. There was a strong, sickly smell of beer and the floor was sticky.

Reeves now knew that it was the time to explain the riddle. "Let me tell you what happened," he said kindly, "but I must be quick. We may not have much time."

CHAPTER 12

"When I used to live and work here," he began, "a very strange-looking man often came in for a drink and occasionally some lunch. I don't remember his name but it is not important. I became suspicious of him because he always seemed to come down the stairs to this part of the building, where the toilets and the cellars are."

"Weak bladder?" asked Archie's Dad, half-joking and half-serious.

"That is what I thought at first," agreed Reeves, "that he was just someone who needed to go to the toilet a lot. But when he started coming every day and spending more and more time down here I became suspicious and one day followed him into these cellars."

"What was he doing?" asked Archie, completely fascinated.

"He was a smuggler, Archie," Reeves said with a clear feeling of anger. "He was receiving strange, and I imagine stolen, goods. RIGHT UNDER MY NOSE!"

"How could he be a smuggler?" asked Archie. "I thought that only happened by the sea. And what was he smuggling? Gold?" He was remembering all the stories of smugglers he had read before.

"Look down there," Reeves instructed Archie and his Dad. "There is your answer."

On the floor in front of them was something that looked like a trap-door covering a hole. It was approximately one-metre-long on all four sides and seemed a mixture of iron and rotten wood.

"A trap-door covering a passage?" enquired Archie's Dad.

"Exactly so," replied Reeves. "That simple looking trap-door is how he used to receive his secret goods. You see, apparently the passage behind that trap door runs in one direction to the River Thames and in another direction directly underneath Aldgate Station, where we have just been."

"You mean that the passage runs directly to where you and your wife were buried and where you think she is now?" asked Archie.

"That is what I was told, by the smuggler himself. The day that I followed him down to these cellars I caught him red-handed just as he was emerging from the passage with a large sack of goods," said Reeves, stroking his beard more and more intensely.

"Wow!" gasped Archie. "He must have been very surprised to see you standing here when he came out of the passage."

"Surprised, and very worried," nodded Reeves. "At that time the Civil War was soon to start and people were betraying lots of people who were not on their side."

Archie thought back to his project on the English Civil War that started in 1642 and remembered the huge struggle for power between Oliver Cromwell and Charles I.

"In fact, the smuggler was so worried that he begged me not to report him to the authorities," continued Reeves. "He probably would have either been put in prison or sent to a Hospital for 'mad' people called Old Bethlem, which used to be exactly where Liverpool Street Station now is."

Archie knew, of course, that Liverpool Street station was just one stop from Aldgate, so it was very close. He immediately thought again about the statue of Venus at Liverpool Station and of Felicity. He was shaken out of his thoughts by the voice of Reeves once more.

"He offered me a deal," Reeves said. "He promised that if I didn't report him to the authorities, he would leave and never use the cellar again. In addition, he would give me the special code that only he knew, which would then open the trap-door."

Archie and his Dad looked at each other, as the story became more and more strange, yet also more exciting.

"I agreed. He left and I never saw him again," concluded Reeves.

"I assume you still know the code?" asked Archie's Dad.

"Well, this is exactly the problem, Mr Balde. He told me the code, but in the form of a riddle. He then disappeared and to this day I not been able to work out its meaning. It didn't bother me too much at first. What would I need with a dirty underground passage? But when I became separated from my wife, I remembered that he told me that this passage runs past where she might be, because it runs directly underneath Aldgate Station in one direction."

For a moment, Archie had a horrible feeling that his Dad would start singing a 'One Direction' song, but fortunately what he did say was more serious for once.

"So let me try and sum this up," Archie's Dad, biting his lip once more. "You have been searching for your wife for over 100 years. You have heard the stories of a ghost – a kind 'Elderly Angel' – helping people at Aldgate station and you are convinced it is her." Archie's Dad paused and looked at Reeves, who nodded, so he kept going. "You travel back and forth on the Metropolitan Line hoping to see her but with no luck, and you think that you need to look underneath Aldgate station, where you were both buried. The problem is that the only way back there is through this passage, but you can't open the trap-door until you solve the riddle given you by the smuggler. Is that correct?" asked Archie's Dad, wiping his brow and pausing to sit on one of the beer barrels, promptly leading to two large stains on his trousers. "Goodness I need a rest. And a drink. And the toilet, it seems," he said, looking at the wet patches on his trousers.

"That is exactly the case, Mr Balde!" replied Reeves, ignoring the comment about the toilet. "I travel back and forth from Aldgate to Harrow-on-the-Hill just looking for clues and that is how I was lucky enough to meet you. Once we spoke and you could see and hear me I knew that you could help."

CHAPTER 13

Archie couldn't help feeling sorry for this poor, lonely ghost. "You must have felt so sad and lonely, especially if you have had no-one to talk to for all these years," he said to Reeves.

Reeves smiled knowingly. "Life is, in many ways, like this Underground Tube Challenge that you are taking, Archie. I couldn't help overhearing your conversations with your friend, Felicity. You see, life is full of both light and colour and feelings of happiness, but also darkness and tunnels and feelings of sadness. Our purpose is to help and support people on their own life journeys, no matter how different they look or think or feel. That is exactly what you did with your friend when you gave her the book and apple juice when she said she was afraid of tunnels."

Not being one for compliments, and not knowing how to explain that Felicity certainly wouldn't describe herself as his friend, Archie paused, remembering that he had told Felicity that 57 % of the London Underground was actually *overground*.

"Does that mean that 57% of our life should be happy and 43% of our life unhappy?" asked Archie, confused. "Like you just said about life being both happiness and sadness?"

Reeves smiled fondly again at Archie's reasoning. "It's not quite like that. Life is a funny thing, Archie," he said. "We certainly can't feel happy all the time. Anyone with a kind heart will have times of feeling sad and hurt. That's very natural. But even in those dark times - those 'tunnels' - we must remember that we will soon emerge into the overground again. As you said to Felicity, 'it's not all tunnels'."

Reeves paused and smiled, before adding: "Being underground doesn't mean being unhappy. It just gives you an opportunity to think more deeply about your journey in life."

Archie looked down again, thinking carefully about Reeves' words. For some reason, he thought back to the time when he owned his first cat, Mars – a beautiful, fluffy, black and white cat that used to sleep under his duvet at night, summer and winter. Archie knew that Mars wouldn't live forever – he was aware that cats' lives are much shorter than humans – and for a time he didn't want to love Mars too much in case he would be too sad when the cat eventually died. But he decided it would be wrong not to love Mars as much as possible while he was still alive. Archie understood, too, that when the happy times did end, then love meant also accepting the bad times: it was about the good times and the bad times, the overground and the underground. He thought again about Reeves' recent words and nodded to himself in agreement. He didn't know how yet, but he knew he desperately wanted to help his new, ghostly friend.

"Archie, believe me, I would love to talk more with you," said Reeves, interrupting Archie's thoughts, "really I would, but I am concerned about what would happen if someone came down here and found us. They wouldn't see me, but they would see you – and you, Mr Balde – and you may end up in trouble. It is time I tell you the riddle." Reeves cleared his ghostly throat. "It went like this," he said.

"When Love and Beauty next kiss the Sun
The sealed cover will then come undone."

"What on earth - or wherever you come from - does *that* mean?" exclaimed Archie's Dad. "Are you sure it means anything at all?"

"I must believe that it does mean something, Mr Balde, as without this possible chance..." Reeves broke off, as if the thought of not being able to find his wife again was too upsetting. He composed himself before speaking again.

"When I caught the smuggler, he was hiding all sorts of strange equipment relating to the stars: small telescopes, maps, charts and calculations. It is no surprise to me, therefore, that the rhyme mentions something to do with the Sun, but what exactly it means, I have no idea. This is why I need Archie's help."

CHAPTER 14

Archie thought again about his English teacher, Mr Penfold, and how he told all of his pupils to analyse a poem or rhyme line by line. Archie tried that method now, first in his head and then out loud to his Dad and Reeves:

"When Love and Beauty next kiss the Sun"

He was quite sure that when the smuggler talked about 'Love and Beauty', he meant Venus – she was the goddess of love and beauty. As for 'kissing' the Sun, he was therefore probably talking about the next time the planet Venus would pass in between the Earth and the Sun, so that it looked from Earth like Venus was a small dot crossing the surface of the Sun. Archie knew that this was called the 'transit of Venus'. As Felicity had said, he had actually told the class about this once and he knew from what Reeves had said that the smuggler was very interested in astronomy, the study of the stars and planets. "That must be what he means," thought Archie.

He explained all this to his Dad and to Reeves. "The transit of Venus is very complicated and rare," he continued, "but I think I understand. I remember reading that although one was predicted in 1631, the first one ever observed was actually in 1639."

"1639? That is more or less the time when I caught the smuggler," said Reeves, thinking hard. "It was not long before the Civil War started."

Archie's Dad scratched his head, knowing that what followed would indeed be complicated. He was a Professor of Medieval History, after all, not a Professor of Astronomy or Mathematics.

"Let's take a closer look at the iron covering," Archie's Dad said as he walked across the sticky floor of the cellar, seemingly accepting now that what was happening was *really* happening. "That will surely give us some clues about how to re-open it."

Reeves smiled. "Believe me, Mr Balde, I have tried to open that covering a thousand times but it seems magically sealed. I have studied it for cracks and signs but there is nothing there to help, only a long series of numbers that seem scratched onto the surface. I imagine they are more to do with orders of drinks than with any code to open the covering."

Archie and his Dad looked closely at the covering, which Reeves claimed led to the underground passage, and focussed on the numbers to which Reeves referred. They were rather faded and hard to make out, but Archie's eyes were strong.

"163116391761176918741882200042012," read Archie aloud.

"Yes, but I don't see how they can be relevant. They are just a list of numbers, that's all," said Reeves.

Archie, though, was intrigued. He loved numbers and always tried to see patterns even if there were none. In that case, he would invent his own pattern. That way, numbers would also be meaningful to him even if they made no sense to anyone else. However, even Archie was struggling to find a connection between this long list of numbers. Whatever could they mean?

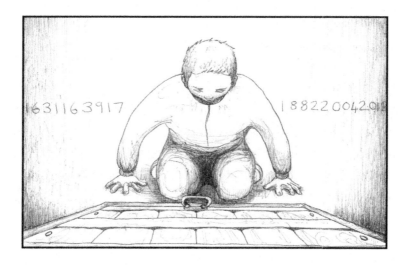

CHAPTER 15

Archie concentrated hard and tried to remember all that he had read about the transit of Venus across the Sun. He thought back to the information he had told the class, even though he was aware that Felicity and her friend Daniella Dufflecoat were laughing at him at the back of the room.

It was all coming back to him now. He knew that transits happened in pairs with a gap of eight years in between and he remembered that the last one was in 2012. That meant there would also have been a transit eight years before, in 2004. "OK," he thought to himself, "I am making progress but all I know is that there were transits in 1631, 1639, 2004 and 2012. That's probably not much to go on."

He felt a little disheartened and worried that he wouldn't be able to help Reeves. Reeves depended on him. He felt that his hands were getting sweaty and his heart pumping very fast again. He breathed deeply and looked again at the numbers on the iron covering, his face almost pressed to the floor.

16311639...

Suddenly, something struck him!

"Look!" exclaimed Archie, staring at the covering. "The code is all the years of the transits of Venus, one after the other. They're all there: 1631 and 1639 – eight years apart. 1761 and 1769 – eight years apart. 1874 and 1882 – eight years apart. 2004 and 2012 – eight years apart! Each year is written one after the other, just without spaces in between. So 2012 was the last one, eight years after 2004."

Archie's Dad was mightily impressed, as always, with his son's knowledge but equally lost in terms of understanding. "So, what does all that mean, Archie?"

Archie said again the rhyme:

"When Love and Beauty next kiss the Sun
The sealed cover will then come undone."

He burst into action again. "We need to scratch the next numbers in the series onto the covering."

Reeves and Archie's Dad both looked puzzled.

"How can we work out the next year in the series?" asked Reeves, bewildered by the turn of events.

Archie closed his eyes and started to calculate in his head. He remembered being fascinated by the very unusual patterns of how often the transit of Venus occurred. He tried to simplify it to himself. "The transits are in a pattern that repeats itself every 243 years, with pairs of transits eight years apart, separated by long gaps of 121.5 years and 105.5 years." He took a deep breath and continued. "The last transit was in 2012, eight years after its previous transit in 2004." He paused. "This pair of transits must therefore belong to the pair of transits that occurred 243 years earlier in 1769 and 1761." He paused again. "The transits after these must have been 105.5 years and 121.5 years later, so 1874 and 1882. 243 years from 1874 is... 2117."

"The year 2117!" exclaimed Archie. "100 years from now!"

Archie quickly looked around him for a piece of stone or flint. His concentration was interrupted by a noise from above them. Someone was coming down the stairs!

CHAPTER 16

"Quickly, Archie! Hide," said his Dad in panic. "Someone's coming! Reeves is OK because no-one else can see him, but you and I will be noticed straightaway!"

"Wait! I just need to scratch in the numbers. There's still time! I can use this," said Archie, holding up a sharp-looking stone.

The steps were getting louder as they descended the stairs. Was it someone going to the toilets or was it the landlord heading directly to where they were in the cellar? How on earth could they explain what they were doing there?

Archie knew he needed to stay calm and concentrate on solving the puzzle. He quickly but carefully scratched the year "2117" onto the covering next to the list of existing numbers.

As he had hoped, the covering was immediately released and opened slightly.

"You've done it!" exclaimed Reeves, ecstatically. "Archie, you have DONE IT!"

Reeves wasted no time. He pulled the covering up as quickly as he could and climbed down. A horribly strong smell of sewage came up from the hole but Reeves didn't seem to mind. When he was in the passage he looked at Archie and his Dad. "I cannot thank you both enough. Now it is time to find Bertha and bring her home." He removed the scarf from his neck and gave it to Archie. "A thank-you gift! Don't forget me, will you?" said Reeves.

"Never," said Archie, with a mixture of excitement and sadness at the realisation that Reeves was about to leave them, seemingly forever.

Reeves smiled. "Now, quick! Hide," he said, as the footsteps had stopped outside the locked cellar door and a jangling of keys could be heard. It was clear that whoever was outside was coming into the cellar.

Reeves slipped into the dark passage below, gently closing the covering behind him so that it would be easy to push it up when he returned with his wife. Archie's Dad quickly grabbed Archie and both of them hid behind a huge barrel of beer.

They were just in time. The cellar door opened and the landlord walked in, his shoes making a squelching sound on the sticky floor. He was whistling quite contently to himself but suddenly stopped, sniffed, shivered, and pulled his cardigan a little tighter around his shoulders. Grabbing a handful of bottles he left the cellar, with the door open so that he could return for more supplies, and headed back upstairs.

Archie and his Dad took this as their chance and left the cellar, past the toilets and up the stairs. As they were reaching the top landing that led back into the bar, they met the landlord again, who was evidently on his way back down to the cellar.

"Still here?" said the landlord, surprised that it was over fifteen minutes since Archie and his Dad had asked to use the toilet.

"Yes," said Archie's Dad, quickly thinking of something to say. "Too much apple juice, I think. Weak bladder."

Archie and his Dad smiled nervously as they passed the landlord, who stared back at them with a puzzled look. They headed straight out of the pub and breathed a huge sigh of relief.

They crossed the road and headed for the Underground. Just as they were about to enter the station, Archie and his Dad noticed a young man sitting on the ground, a small box in front of him with a few pennies inside. He looked cold, hungry, tired and very lonely. He also seemed to be talking to himself. Archie looked with great sympathy at his Dad, who knew exactly what his look meant. These were the modern-day homeless, poor and lonely – just like Reeves. Archie's Dad reached into his pocket and gave some change to Archie, who placed it in the box. The young man smiled gratefully: "Thank you," he said. "Thank you very much."

CHAPTER 17

Archie and his Dad jumped on the first train heading in the direction of Liverpool Street. Archie's Dad checked his watch: "Exactly 12:27," he said. "Reeves was right: we haven't lost a single second! He said time was flexible and that we wouldn't lose a moment. We are back on our Tube Challenge! High-five, Archibald Balde!" Archie looked down, unsure of what was more embarrassing: doing a high-five with his Dad or being called by his full name.

The next few hours were far less eventful. Archie's Dad managed to drop his folder four more times; he sang twice and made numerous unfunny jokes.

Archie felt tired as they crawled along the Central Line towards Epping. Much to his embarrassment, his Dad started loudly humming the theme tune to an old TV programme called 'Grange Hill', just as they arrived at that station.

Not long afterwards, Archie was surprised to see a young girl in tears sitting on her own a little way down the carriage. He was even more surprised to discover that it was Felicity. Felicity! What was she doing there? Where was her Mum? And more importantly, why was she crying?

"Dad, look! It's Felicity from my class over there. She's crying. Come on."

Archie and his Dad headed over to where Felicity was sitting. Tears were streaming down her face.

"Felicity," spoke Archie with genuine concern, "what's

wrong? Why are you crying?"

Felicity looked up and was both surprised and relieved to see Archie and his Dad in front of her.

"I've lost my Mum!" she replied in between heavy sobs.

Archie's heart sank. "Your Mum?" he asked. "Where is she? Did she get off the Tube without you or something?"

Felicity looked at Archie, frustrated that he was saying something that was clearly obvious. "I don't know, Archie. I've lost her. I don't know what to do."

Archie's Dad leaned over and tried to comfort Felicity who was crying again.

"When did you last see your Mum, Felicity?" he asked gently.

Felicity explained how she and her Mum were coming back from Highgate after visiting her great uncle's grave. They were on the train, both reading their books - the one that Archie had given her - when they suddenly realised they were at Moorgate, which was their stop.

"We quickly ran towards the doors but Mum's bag got caught as she got out. As she pulled it, the strap of the bag snapped. I was behind her so I didn't get off while she was trying to rescue her bag. Suddenly, the doors closed and Mum was outside the train but I was still inside. Mum shouted at the train guard but then the train started..." Felicity broke into huge sobs again.

"Sliding doors were first used on the Tube in 1919," said Archie directly.

Felicity looked at him with anger: "I DON'T CARE ABOUT YOUR STUPID TRAINS!" she shouted at Archie, who looked upset by Felicity's outburst.

Archie's Dad felt it was best to intervene. "Felicity," he said. "Don't worry. We'll stay with you until you find your Mum again. Does she have a mobile number?"

"Yes, but I don't know it. I'll never see her again," she said as the sobs came as strong as ever.

"OK. Let's think about this clearly and sensibly," said Archie's Dad. "You were at Moorgate when it happened. That's..." He was looking at the Tube map on the wall directly above Felicity, who was sitting opposite him, and working out how far away they were now.

"Eight stops," said Archie immediately, not needing the map.

"OK," continued Archie's Dad, pleased that his son's Tube knowledge was coming in so handy, "do you and your Mum have any agreed rules on what you should do if ever you become separated anywhere? This is very important."

"Mum tells me that if we ever get separated I should stay exactly where I am, and never talk to strangers except if they are wearing an official uniform," Felicity replied, slightly calmer now that she wasn't alone any more.

"That's good advice, Felicity, and I think your Mum will be doing exactly the right thing," said Archie's Dad.

"What do you mean?" asked Felicity, frowning, but also a little more hopeful.

"I mean that I think your Mum will still be at Moorgate talking to a station guard about what happened. We should take you back there." He turned to look at his son, "I'm afraid we will lose some time on our Tube Challenge then, Archie, as we haven't got Reeves anymore."

"That's fine, Dad. Helping Felicity is much more important," said Archie with a smile.

Felicity smiled back, reassured. "Thank you," she said, sniffing and starting to wipe away her tears. He was a kind boy, she realised. Yes, unusual and very weird, but kind.

When they reached Moorgate station, Felicity was so relieved to see her Mum still on the platform with a train guard that she gave a shout of relief. It sounded like a mix between laughing and crying. She turned to Archie just before leaving the train.

"Oh, and I can come to your birthday party. Thank you for inviting me," she said with a smile.

CHAPTER 18

Archie and his Dad waited until Felicity and her Mum were back together and having a cuddle. They stayed on the train and sat down, feeling relieved that Felicity had found her Mum but also exhausted. Even Archie's Dad was lost for words about what had happened over the last couple of hours.

The silence was broken by the voice of a lady sitting opposite, muttering to herself. She was dressed in bright, clean white trainers, jeans and a baseball cap. Archie knew at once from her accent that she must be American. The man next to her must be her husband, he thought.

The man then spoke up, "I am telling you, Jeannie: I saw something on the tracks."

"Bert Blackstone," replied his wife, exasperated, "you can't even see as far as to zip up your pants, so don't you go telling me your nonsense about seeing some ghost. I knew this London ghost tour of yours was a silly idea. Now you won't sleep for three days and your blood pressure will hit the roof, all because you think you saw an old lady stroking someone's hair. And don't you even get started again on that supposed ghost of a drowned young 11-year-old boy at Highgate Cemetery or the sad old man with funny socks stroking his beard walking down Aldgate High Street. Just don't get started."

"All I am saying is that I saw something, that's all," Bert replied.

Bert thought it safer not to say any more for the moment, but instead continued to look into his book, *Mysteries of the London Underground*.

"What I am more surprised about," piped up Jeannie again, chewing her gum harder and harder, "is why the so-called clever English folk decided to build Big Ben so close to the metro station. They could have moved it back a bit, you know, made more space. I've still got a creaked neck from looking up. And who is Ben anyway? Maybe he's the guy who rings the bells every hour. You listening to me, Bert Blackstone, or am I just talking away to myself, again?"

"Here it is," said Bert, pointing to a page in his book. "Listen, and I'll read it to you, Jeannie:

> *'There's a kind Elderly Angel at Aldgate station. Over a century ago, someone at Aldgate slipped onto a live rail, knocking himself unconscious and sending over 20,000 volts*

through his body. Incredibly, he survived and people who saw the accident say that they saw the shining figure of an old lady kneeling next to him, stroking his hair.'"

Bert continued: "It says there is even a special log-book for ghost sightings at Aldgate station. A 'kind Elderly Angel': well, I'm telling you, that's who I saw."

"Will you just knock it off?" said Jeannie, closing her eyes. "I just want to check into our room and have a lie down. I'm as tired as a Texan sheepdog."

Archie and his Dad looked at each other and smiled. They knew that the 'Elderly Angel' must be Mrs Reeves. "Mr Reeves said that she was such a kind lady. And we know that she's been stuck underground at Aldgate. It *must* have been her who helped that person," whispered Archie to his Dad.

Archie's Dad nodded his head in wonder. "You know what, Archie, I think you may be right. I just hope he manages to find her again and take her back home."

CHAPTER 19

The rest of the day was rather straightforward compared with what had gone before: no more encounters with Reeves or Felicity, just an annoying passenger with her dog, who took a fancy to the smell of Archie's Dad's uneaten salami sandwiches and the laces on Archie's shoes. That and lots of wonderful Tube trains for Archie to ride on, maps to examine, timetables to check, and numbers to think about. But nothing quite matched the excitement of the morning.

By the time they emerged from the exit of Heathrow Terminal 5 it was past midnight. They were both extremely tired but full of wonder at the day they had experienced and the people they had met. No, they hadn't broken the world record, mainly because Archie's Dad had lost his Oyster Card somewhere along the Piccadilly Line and they had lost precious time. But Archie didn't care. The memories he now had and the knowledge he had gained would stay with him longer than any world record.

"Come on, let's get that taxi over there and head home to bed," said Archie's Dad wearily as they slowly walked towards the black car. To their astonishment, the driver was the same one that had taken them to Chesham at 4.30am the morning before. The driver recognised them at once.

"Bit late, innit?" the driver asked.

"Yes, we didn't break the record but completed the Challenge in 19 hours and 4 minutes," said Archie as he climbed into the back with his Dad.

"I think that's amazing," said the taxi driver. "Well done."

Archie smiled with pride.

"Same address as this morning?" asked the driver to Archie's Dad. "I should still have it in my sat nav."

"Yes, please," replied Archie's Dad, with a yawn.

As the taxi drove off, Archie's Dad reached his arm around Archie's shoulder. "I am so proud of you, son," he spoke with such warmth in his eyes.

Archie smiled and looked back at his Dad. "I am so proud of you too, Dad."

Archie's Dad threw his other arm around Archie, forgetting he was holding his folder, which promptly caught the top of Archie's head.

"Most of the time, anyway," said Archie rubbing his head before laying it on his Dad's shoulder.

He was tired. What a day it had been. He couldn't wait to tell his Mum and little sister all about it. But would they believe him? Most of what had happened was truly *unbelievable*. And what about Felicity? Should he tell her? What if she just thought he was being strange and weird again and decide *not* to come to his birthday party after all? He couldn't risk that. He had already made a mental note to make sure there would be plenty of egg sandwiches present. And serviettes.

Archie had learnt again how everyone is different, but still essentially the same, with a good heart. Everyone has their own hopes and fears and they often cover them up so no one can see. He knew he was different but being different does not make you mad. It just makes you different!

He thought about how much life is like a journey; people need to stop, look and listen more. Talking to Felicity had made him realise that people are sometimes cruel and unkind because they are scared or insecure. He remembered that there are many tunnels in life and we all need to make our way through as best as we can. He had found his own way: Archie's Way. "Maybe Felicity is a little bit like the planet Venus," he thought to himself in his unique way, recalling that an atmosphere of thick cloud stopped anyone from really seeing the surface of the planet. Maybe Felicity's cruelty was her own 'atmosphere' - just a lot of hot air - but if you looked beyond that you could see the real person.

He was too tired to think any more. His eyes were heavy and he drifted into a pleasant sleep, thinking about trains, Reeves, Mrs Reeves, Felicity, and all the other wonderful people he had met. His dream was suddenly interrupted by the voice of the taxi driver.

"I had Tim Henman in the back last week," he said, looking in his mirror.

Archie looked at his Dad, smiled, closed his eyes again and rested his head back on his Dad's shoulder, his hand tightly clutching Reeves' scarf covering the scar on his hand. Noticing that Archie's eyes were closed, his Dad leaned forward and spoke quietly to the driver: "Tell me more about Kylie Minogue…"

CHAPTER 20

Archie's Dad awoke early the next morning, wanting to make sure that Archie didn't oversleep for school. No inset day today. As usual, he made his coffee and checked the news on his phone. His beloved football team, West Ham, had lost last night - again. He sighed, buttered his toast on both sides by mistake, and then read something on a news blog that made him dribble his coffee:

> "*An American couple demanded to leave their accommodation at the Hoop and Grapes pub in Aldgate last night after claiming their room was haunted. Bert and Jeannie Blackstone, on holiday from Texas, claimed that two ghostly figures - an elderly man and woman - had tried to climb into the same bed as them in their attic room, saying that it was their home and that they had waited a long time to climb into bed and sleep. According to Mr Blackstone, 'the woman had shiny grey hair and the man had long hair and a beard. He also wore dirty socks and smelt like he had come up from a sewer.'*"

THE END

Printed in Great Britain
by Amazon

40391540R00046